Finding the Golden Ruler

LITTLE SIMON INSPIRATIONS

An imprint of Simon & Schuster Children's Publishing Division
1230 Avenue of the Americas, New York, New York 10020
Text copyright © 2005 by Karen Hill
Illustrations copyright © 2005 by Felicia Hoshino
All rights reserved, including the right of reproduction
in whole or in part in any form.
LITTLE SIMON INSPIRATIONS and associated colophon
are trademarks of Simon & Schuster, Inc.
Manufactured in the United States of America
First Edition
2 4 6 8 10 9 7 5 3 1
ISBN 1-4169-0513-8
Scripture quoted from *The Message*, copyright © 1993
by Eugene Peterson (Colorado Springs, CO: Navpress),
and *New American Standard Bible*, copyright © 1995
(La Habra, CA: The Lockman Foundation).

Finding the Golden Ruler

By **Karen Hill**

Illustrated by **Felicia Hoshino**

LITTLE SIMON INSPIRATIONS

New York London Toronto Sydney

For my son John: "Sing, sing your heart
out to God . . . thanking God the Father
every step of the way." (COL. 3: 16)
—K. H.

For Mom and Dad,
with much love —F. H.

"Treat people the same way you want them to treat you." (Matthew 7: 12)

John could not find what he was looking for. He searched everywhere. He opened his toy box and looked inside. He peeked under the bed. He looked behind his stack of favorite storybooks.

He lifted up the sofa cushions and looked underneath. He even squeezed behind the washing machine to see if it was there.

"It's not here," he said to himself.

John dashed out the back door and scrambled
to the tip-tip-top of his tree house.

"Hmm. It's not here, either," he mumbled.

"What'd you say?" asked Dad, raking leaves
in the yard below.

"It's not up here," called John.

"What's not here?" Dad asked.

But John was too busy to answer. He had already scurried down from the tree and was racing toward the doghouse.

Lazy old Annabelle dozed on the grass. She woke up to see John poke his head into her doghouse.

"Woof . . . woof," Annabelle happily greeted her pal, hoping for a pat on the head or maybe even one of those yummy doggie treats her owner always kept in his pocket.

But John was too busy to think about pats on the head or doggie treats.

"It's not in your house, Annabelle," John said, running back to the house.

The big old dog gave a yawning "woof" and went back to her nap.

"Where could it be?" John thought. Now he was in the kitchen, looking under the sink.

"Have you fed your fish today?" asked Mom.

"Too busy," replied John. "I'm looking."

"Looking for what?" Mom asked.

"I'm searching for the golden ruler," John said.
"It must be here somewhere."

"Golden ruler? We don't have a golden ruler,"
said Mom.

Puzzled, John flopped on the floor, tired from his quest. "But my teacher said that everyone has one. And she told us we should always use it. So I'm looking for *my* golden ruler so that I can use it."

Mom smiled. "I think your teacher meant to say 'golden rule.'"

"Yes, that's what she said. Golden rule. Where is ours?"

"The golden rule isn't a measuring stick. It's something in your heart," Mom told John. "The golden rule is the best way to live—it means this: Treat others the way you want them to treat you."

John thought about that. "But how do I use
the golden rule?" he asked.

"The best way is to think about others before
we think about ourselves," Mom replied. "Look
around and think of ways to treat others the way
you like to be treated."

"I know!" John shouted. He jumped up
and opened the pantry door.

He grabbed a can off the shelf and climbed
on the counter by his fish.

He poured just a pinch of fish food into the fishbowl.

"Here, little pal. Here's your breakfast. Sorry I didn't bring it sooner."

Mom went back to her baking. John started out the back door but stopped. He ran back and gave Mom a big hug.

"Thanks, Mom. I'm going outside to use my golden ruler, I mean, golden *rule*!"

Out in the yard Annabelle still napped. John
sat down beside her quietly and began to stroke
her furry head.

"Good doggie," he said, "good girl."

Annabelle wagged her tail.

"How about a little doggie treat?" John asked
as he reached into his pocket.

John and Annabelle played awhile. Then John saw his dad still raking leaves.

"Hey, Dad," John yelled. "Can I help you?"

Mom was watching through the kitchen window.

"Looks like John found his golden ruler after all," she said and smiled.